DEAR MOUSE FRIENDS, WELCOME TO THE

STONE AGE!

WELCOME TO THE STONE AGE . . . AND THE WORLD OF THE CAVEMICE!

CAPITAL: OLD MOUSE CITY

POPULATION: WE'RE NOT SURE. (MATH DOESN'T EXIST YET!) BUT BESIDES CAVEMICE, THERE ARE PLENTY OF DINOSAURS, <u>WAY</u> TOO MANY SABER-TOOTHED TIGERS, AND FEROCIOUS CAVE BEARS — BUT NO MOUSE HAS EVER HAD THE COURAGE TO COUNT THEM!

TYPICAL FOOD: PETRIFIED CHEESE SOUP

NATIONAL HOLIDAY: GREAT ZAP DAY, WHICH CELEBRATES THE DISCOVERY OF FIRE. RODENTS EXCHANGE GRILLED CHEESE SANDWICHES ON THIS HOLIDAY.

NATIONAL DRINK: MAMMOTH MILKSHAKES

CLIMATE: Unpredictable, WITH FREQUENT METEOR SHOWERS

cheese soup

milkshake

MONEY

SEASHELLS OF ALL SHAPES AND SIZES

MEASUREMENT

THE BASIC UNIT OF MEASUREMENT IS BASED ON THE LENGTH OF THE TAIL OF THE LEADER OF THE VILLAGE. A UNIT CAN BE DIVIDED INTO A HALF TAIL OR QUARTER TAIL. THE LEADER IS ALWAYS READY TO PRESENT HIS TAIL WHEN THERE IS A DISPUTE.

THE CAVEMICE

Geronimo

Trap

Thea

Benjamin

Bugsy Wugsy

Hercule Poirat

Grandma Ratrock

Geronimo Stilton

MY AUTOSAURUS WILL WIN!

Scholastic Inc.

Copyright © 2012 by Edizioni Piemme S.p.A., Palazzo Mondadori, Via Mondadori 1, 20090 Segrate, Italy. International Rights © Atlantyca S.p.A. English translation © 2016 by Atlantyca S.p.A.

The publisher does not have any control over and does not assume any responsibility for author or third-party websites or their content.

GERONIMO STILTON names, characters, and related indicia are copyright, trademark, and exclusive license of Atlantyca S.p.A. All rights reserved. The moral right of the author has been asserted. Based on an original idea by Elisabetta Dami. www.geronimostilton.com

Published by Scholastic Inc., *Publishers since 1920,* 557 Broadway, New York, NY 10012. SCHOLASTIC and associated logos are trademarks and/or registered trademarks of Scholastic Inc.

Stilton is the name of a famous English cheese. It is a registered trademark of the Stilton Cheese Makers' Association. For more information, go to www.stiltoncheese.com.

No part of this publication may be reproduced, stored in a retrieval system, or transmitted in any form or by any means, electronic, mechanical, photocopying, recording, or otherwise, without written permission of the copyright holder. For information regarding permission, please contact: Atlantyca S.p.A., Via Leopardi 8, 20123 Milan, Italy; e-mail foreignrights@atlantyca.it, www.atlantyca.com.

This book is a work of fiction. Names, characters, places, and incidents are either the product of the author's imagination or are used fictitiously, and any resemblance to actual persons, living or dead, business establishments, events, or locales is entirely coincidental.

ISBN 978-0-545-87246-1

Text by Geronimo Stilton
Original title *Mi si è bucato il trottosauro!*
Cover by Flavio Ferron
Illustrations by Giuseppe Facciotto (design) and Daniele Verzini (color)
Graphics by Marta Lorini

Special thanks to Tracey West
Translated by Julia Heim
Interior design by Becky James

10 9 8 7 6 5 4 3 2 1   16 17 18 19 20

Printed in the U.S.A.   40
First printing 2016

MANY AGES AGO, ON PREHISTORIC MOUSE ISLAND, THERE
WAS A VILLAGE CALLED OLD MOUSE CITY. IT WAS INHABITED
BY BRAVE *RODENT SAPIENS* KNOWN AS THE CAVEMICE.
DANGERS SURROUNDED THE MICE AT EVERY TURN:
EARTHQUAKES, METEOR SHOWERS, FEROCIOUS DINOSAURS,
AND FIERCE GANGS OF SABER-TOOTHED TIGERS. BUT THE
BRAVE CAVEMICE FACED IT ALL WITH A SENSE OF HUMOR,
AND WERE ALWAYS READY TO LEND A HAND TO OTHERS.
HOW DO I KNOW THIS? I DISCOVERED AN
ANCIENT BOOK WRITTEN BY MY ANCESTOR, GERONIMO
STILTONOOT! HE CARVED HIS STORIES INTO STONE TABLETS
AND ILLUSTRATED THEM WITH HIS ETCHINGS.
I AM PROUD TO SHARE THESE STONE AGE STORIES WITH
YOU. THE EXCITING ADVENTURES OF THE CAVEMICE WILL
MAKE YOUR FUR STAND ON END, AND THE JOKES WILL
TICKLE YOUR WHISKERS! HAPPY READING!

Geronimo Stilton

WARNING! DON'T IMITATE THE CAVEMICE.
WE'RE NOT IN THE STONE AGE ANYMORE!

WHAT A STONE-AGE STENCH!

It was a hot summer night as my sister, Thea, and I walked through *Old Mouse City*. When we reached the port, we stopped to admire the **SUNSET** over the ocean.

The sun reminded me of a wheel of **orange cheddar**, and my stomach rumbled. Thea and I quickly headed into the ꞦƟƬƬƎꞥ ƬƟƟƬH ƬꞥVEꞥꞥ, owned by my cousin Trap and his friend Greasella Stonyfur. The place was famouse throughout the city for its excellent **food** and its warm and welcoming atmosphere.

It was no coincidence that Thea and I had walked to the tavern at dinnertime. You might not believe this, but Trap had actually invited us there for a FREE meal! Trap **never** gives away anything for free. So this was a pretty BIG DEAL!

When we arrived, Trap greeted us with a big smile.

"**My dear cousins!**" he exclaimed. "How nice to see you. Greasella has prepared

a mountain of **cheesy** macaroni for you that will make you lick your whiskers!"

A mountain of macaroni? For free? That was not like Trap at all. He was acting **very strange** . . .

Before I could question him, he placed a **CHISEL** in my paw and pushed me in front of a little mouse who was having dinner with his family.

"**GERONIMO STILTONOOT**," Trap began solemnly, "let me introduce Squirt, a young friend of mine who has something to ask you."

The young mouse **timidly** approached me, holding a tiny slab of stone in his paws.

"Are you r-really G-Geronimo Stiltonoot?" he asked **nervously**.

"Yes," I answered. "It's really me."

The little mouse **blushed**. "How

exciting! The editor of *The Stone Gazette*, the most famouse newspaper of the Stone Age, is here in front of me! Could . . . could I *please* have your autograph?"

I am always happy to give my **fans** what they want (especially when I find out that I have fans!). So I etched an **autograph** for him and then Thea and I sat down at our table.

It's really you!

5

Trap and Greasella overloaded our table with plates of food! We each ate:

- **7 ENCHILADAS** stuffed with swamp grass and swimming in cheese sauce;

- **11 BALLS** of mammoth mozzarella;

- **14 PLATES** of cheesy macaroni;

- **21 CHEESE DUMPLINGS** on a bed of kale; and

- **5 CUPS** of ricotta ice cream topped with fossilized berries!

It was the most DELICIOUS Paleolithic dinner I had ever eaten!

BURRP!P!

I felt like I had swallowed a **BOULDER**! But Trap wasn't done. He brought us one last SURPRISE dish.

"**NO MORE**, Trap, please," said Thea, exhausted from all the feasting.

"I couldn't eat another bite!" I protested.

But we quickly realized that Trap had brought us something really, really special!

Burp!

Burp!

Trap set a platter in front of us, and a familiar STENCH spread throughout the tavern. Thea and I exchanged stunned glances. There was only one thing in all of Old Mouse City that smelled like that: VOLCANICO CHEESE!

It is a special cheese made with **hot lava** peppers that only grow in Boulder Bay.

VOLCANICO

INGREDIENTS

SOUR MILK

HOT LAVA PEPPERS

FRESH WATER (TO PUT OUT THE FIRE!)

"Attention, cousins!" said Trap. "These are the very last TWO CHUNKS of Volcanico in all of Old Mouse City!"

Volcanico is so RARE and wonderful that Thea and I could not resist. We ate it very slowly, savoring every bite. Oh, what a treat!

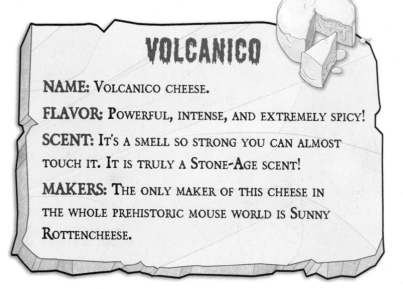

VOLCANICO

NAME: VOLCANICO CHEESE.

FLAVOR: POWERFUL, INTENSE, AND EXTREMELY SPICY!

SCENT: IT'S A SMELL SO STRONG YOU CAN ALMOST TOUCH IT. IT IS TRULY A STONE-AGE SCENT!

MAKERS: THE ONLY MAKER OF THIS CHEESE IN THE WHOLE PREHISTORIC MOUSE WORLD IS SUNNY ROTTENCHEESE.

FIVE HUNDRED SHELLS!

I still couldn't believe it. Trap, my **GREEDY** cousin, had given us the last two pieces of Volcanico instead of eating them himself! I was touched.

"You are so sweet, Trap!" I cried, jumping up to hug him. "You truly have a heart of gold!"

So sweet!

But Thea stared at Trap suspiciously.

"Enough with the sweetness, Geronimo," she said. "**SOMETHING'S UP**. Trap, you need to tell us

what's behind all this!"

Trap smiled innocently. "Can't I just be nice to my cousins?" he asked. "And besides, I have a **reeeallly smaaaall** surprise for you."

I jumped.

"SURPRISE? WHAT SURPRISE?"

When Trap uses the word *surprise*, I can always smell **TROUBLE** coming.

"L-l-let me explain," he said nervously.

He took a few steps back from Thea. (She was clearly **ANGRY**, and you don't want to **mess** with Thea when she's angry!)

"Do you know Sunny

What are you up to?

Rottencheese?" he asked.

Sunny Rottencheese. That name sounded familiar.

"Of course I do," Thea replied. "She is the only rodent in Old Mouse City who knows the recipe for Volcanico."

Trap nodded. "Exactly! So, Sunny was about to make another **BATCH** of Volcanico when she discovered a **problem**."

"What problem?" I asked. "Don't keep us in **SUSPENSE**!"

"The problem was that she ran out of an essential **ingredient**: hot lava peppers! So she decided to announce a **competition**," Trap said.

Thea and I looked at each other, curious.

"The rules are simple," Trap continued. "Contestants must travel to **BOULDER BAY** on an **AUTOSAURUS**, get some **lava peppers**, and then return to Old Mouse City. Any contestant who returns with peppers will get a **GIANT WHEEL** of Volcanico from Sunny!"

"A giant wheel!" I repeated.

"That's not all," continued Trap. "The first to cross the finish line will get:

FIVE HUNDRED SHELLS!

All to be spent at the amazing Rottencheese cheese shop." His eyes sparkled. "**Five hundred shells!** Can you imagine?"

Five hundred shells!

He rubbed his paws together. "By the Great Zap! If I **won**, I could stock my tavern with cheese for a whole year!"

"So why don't you enter the competition?" I asked encouragingly.

Trap **slapped** me on the back. "Ah, I knew you wouldn't let me down, cousin!" he said. "You're always up for an **adventure**!"

"Wait just one minute —" I began, but Thea interrupted me.

"**OF COURSE!**" she exclaimed, clearly excited. "I'm going to enter, too! **BOULDER BAY** is so far away, and has barely been explored . . . **imagine** what we'll find there! Let's sign up right now!"

"***ABSOLUTELY NOT!***" I protested. "You two can go, but leave me out of it!"

Trap **ignored** me. "So it's all three of us, then!" he said happily. "I'll go sign us up right now."

*"**YOU'RE NOT LISTENING TO ME! I SAID I AM NOT GOING!**"* I yelled right in his ear. But Trap pretended he didn't hear me.

"GREAT ROCKY BOULDERS, THIS IS GOING TO BE THE MOST MOUSETASTIC COMPETITION IN THE STONE AGE!".

UH-OH . . . SMELLS LIKE TROUBLE!

NO, NO, NO! I would not let them **drag** me off on another adventure. There was no way I was going to risk extinction in a bay all the way at the end of the prehistoric world just to win some cheese — even if it was really good cheese!

Trap and Thea weren't worried about the DANGER at all.

"First, we need to prepare the AUTOSAURUSES," Trap said. Autosauruses are how we cavemice get around quickly. "Geronimo, go get yours," he said.

"Mine?" I asked. "Why aren't we taking *your* autosaurus?"

"We can't," Trap moaned. "His feet are all **worn out**. I had to take him to the dino repairmouse! He won't be ready until next week, and the race starts **tomorrow morning** at dawn!"

AHA! That's why Trap was being so nice! The free dinner, the autograph, the

Volcanico — it all made sense. Trap needed me for my autosaurus!

"Come on, cousin," Trap said. "I know that **DEEP**, **DEEP** down you want to come with us. Once we win the race, it will be raining **shells** for all of us! I mean, especially for me, but at least it will stay in the **family**, right?"

Thea had a different point. "Also, it's a great opportunity to **ETCH** an amazing article about Boulder Bay," she added.

"**Article?**" I asked. "I won't be able to etch any article. Do you know why?"

"Why?" asked Trap.

"Because I won't be able

to write an article when I'm **extinct**!" I shouted.

I was determined not to go — not even if our village leader, **Ernest Heftymouse**, asked me in person.

Just as I had that thought, an all-too-familiar voice **SURPRISED** me from behind. **"Geronimo Stiltonoot!"**

I couldn't believe it! It was the voice of . . .

"Old Mouse City is so **proud** of you,

You will win, Stiltonoot!

Geronimo," said Ernest Heftymouse (yes, it was really him). "We know that you're going to win!"

Then the village leader squeezed me in a mammoth hug. He almost crushed my bones!

Remember that TROUBLE I smelled earlier? Now it was stinking worse than the smelliest cheese!

21

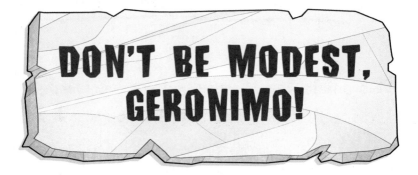

DON'T BE MODEST, GERONIMO!

When I recovered from Ernest's hug, I realized there was a MOUSE standing next to him with a big smile on her face. She wore a white scarf around her neck and looked very friendly.

"This is Sunny Rottencheese," said Ernest. "She's the most EXPERT cheese maker in the whole Stone Age, and the only one who knows the original recipe for Volcanico. She is the organizer of this competition."

Sunny thrust out her paw and vigorously shook Thea's paw and then mine.

"This is the famouse Geronimo

Stiltonoot!" Ernest explained to Sunny. He put his arm around me like we were two old friends. "Geronimo is leading one of the teams from Old Mouse City!"

Grrr . . .

I **GLARED** at Trap, and he smiled like there was nothing wrong. But there was! He had spread the word that I was entering the *RACE* before I had even accepted! I was so **ANGRY** that I wouldn't have been surprised if *smoke* poured from my ears!

Then I realized that everyone was **STARING** at me.

I started to protest. **"But I —"**

Thea clapped her over my mouth. "Don't be modest, Geronimo. We all know

24

how **excited** you are to enter the race."

Sunny Rottencheese **smiled** at me.

"I had no doubt!" she exclaimed. "I have heard a lot about the **great adventures** of the Stiltonoot family. Especially you, Geronimo."

Then Ernest **ELBOWED** me, almost knocking me over.

Well . . .

I'm a big fan!

25

"Miss Rottencheese is a **big fan** of yours," he told me. "She always reads *The Stone Gazette* to keep up on the **latest** news!"

Sunny nodded, **blushing**. "In fact," she said with a sigh, "if I'm being HONEST, I came to the tavern tonight just to meet you! And, well, if you could give me an autograph . . ."

I am the happiest mouse in the Stone Age!

I was as **petrified** as a stone wall. Sunny Rottencheese was famouse for her **masterful** cheese-making skills. And *she* wanted an autograph from *me*? I had never encountered so many ADMIRERS in one day. So, for the second time that night, I ETCHED my name. What an honor!

"I just can't wait to tell my friends that you are taking part in the competition!" Sunny said, grinning. "Oh, today I am the happiest mouse in all of the Stone Age!"

How could I say no to such a sweet and friendly admirer? It looked like I was on my way to Boulder Bay, whether I liked it or not.

Ernest winked at me. "If you win the race, I'll make sure my lovely daughter, Harriet, is there to congratulate you."

GULP!
THAT'S ALL I NEEDED!

Now, Harriet is a perfectly nice rodent. But her LOUD personality is as STRONG as blue cheese, and I am more of a mild mozzarella. We just don't MIX.

And that's the problem. Harriet has a **crush** on me, but my heart beats for another rodent. The most intelligent, beautiful, fascinating, tough, and brave rodent in all of the Stone Age: Clarissa Conjurat, the daughter of Bluster, our village shaman.

Hmm . . . maybe if I won the race, Clarissa would be **IMPRESSED** with me! I could picture myself looking into her **EYES**

Harriet Heftymouse

28

as we sat down to eat two chunks of Volcanico . . .

Oh, what a dream!

OH, WHAT A MOUSE!

The thought of a romantic evening with Clarissa made me change my mind. And because I was doing Trap a favor, I decided to ask him for a free dinner for two at his tavern.

"I'll do it!" I exclaimed. "But on one condition . . ."

"**I KNEW IT!**" Ernest blurted out. "You read my mind."

I frowned, confused. "What do you mean?"

"You were about to say that you will write an **article** about the race!" he said.

I gulped. "Well, actually . . ."

"Oh, **WHAT A MOUSE** you are, Geronimo Stiltonoot!" Ernest said, and he **squeezed** my paw and shook it hard. "Imagine, volunteering to work even when you are in the middle of a **DANGEROUS** competition."

I sighed. **Nobody** was listening to me today!

GREAT! Now, besides having to race

Oh, what a mouse!

to my almost certain **extinction**, I had to etch a detailed article about some *silly* autosaurus race. What had Trap *dragged* me into?

Ernest gave me one last **slap** on the back.

"I'm so glad you **volunteered**, Geronimo," he said. "If you hadn't, I would have **ORDERED** you to do it myself!"

SO GLAD YOU VOLUNTEERED?

I almost wanted to cry. Why was nobody listening to me?

But I knew I had to go through with it. Ernest was so **PROUD** of me that he was **puffing out** his chest like he had captured the terrible Tiger Khan, leader of the saber-toothed tigers, with his own paws.

Next to him, Sunny was **smiling** so hard that she was practically beaming!

Trap looked as **happy** as a rat in a cheese cave, and Thea's eyes were shining with excitement.

I sighed and gave in to my **fate**. I was going to Boulder Bay, whether I wanted to or not!

We said good-bye to one another and made a plan to meet the next morning in

Singing Rock Square. From there, we would depart for the *RACE*.

And so, feeling as low as a baby dinosaur whose bone has been taken away, I returned home.

WHAT A BAD NIGHT!

READY . . . SET . . .

The next morning, as the sun rose, a crowd gathered in Singing Rock Square. Every rodent in Old Mouse City was excited about the competition. Getting to watch the start of the RACE was almost as exciting as being **CHASED** by a saber-toothed tiger — and a lot safer, too.

As the crowd looked on, seven TEAMS lined up on the starting line:

THEA ON GRUNTY, HER TURBO VELOCIRAPTOR AUTOSAURUS;

THE FAMOUSE RACING DRIVER DASH DINOMOUSE, ON HIS SPEEDSAURUS 3000;

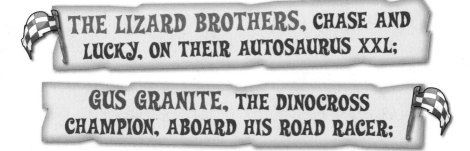

THE LIZARD BROTHERS, CHASE AND LUCKY, ON THEIR AUTOSAURUS XXL;

GUS GRANITE, THE DINOCROSS CHAMPION, ABOARD HIS ROAD RACER;

JACK PRONTO, DRIVING A SPORTSAURUS;

TINA SCURRYTAIL AND GINA SPRINTSTONE, ON THEIR RALLYSAURUS;

AND FINALLY . . . ME AND TRAP, ON MY LAZY CITY AUTOSAURUS.

Sigh. I would much rather have been back in my cave, **snuggled** in bed, *snoring* peacefully and *dreaming* of cheese. But that was not to be.

Trap was preparing for the race by eating a dozen **cream cheese** donuts. I was

feeding my autosaurus an extra-large super-fruity **smoothie** with red onion juice. It's the only way to get him to focus.

As soon as we were all ready, Ernest Heftymouse held up a checkered flag.

"READY . . . SET . . ."

But a voice interrupted him.

"Geronimooooo . . . Show them what you've got!"

It was none other than Clarissa Conjurat! She was waving a PINK handkerchief at me.

My whiskers trembled at the sight of her.

Oh, what a rodent!

"I'm rooting for you!" Clarissa yelled encouragingly. "Because you always lose!"

Okay . . . so she wasn't cheering for me because she thought I was the most **HANDSOME** or **STRONGEST** rodent in the race. But at least she was cheering for me! I was floating on a cloud until I noticed that the other racers were scowling at me.

BONES AND STONES, CLARISSA HAD INTERRUPTED THE START!

I was so **embarrassed** that I wanted to disappear! Ernest shot me an **annoyed**

look and then waved his checkered flag again.

"READY . . . SET . . . GO!"

All the teams **CHARGED** forward with an **uproar** that sounded louder than a herd of angry mammoths!

Thea Stiltonoot
QUALITIES: ADVENTUROUS AND BRAVE, SHE NEVER BACKS DOWN FROM A CHALLENGE.
AUTOSAURUS: GRUNTY, A BABY TURBO VELOCIRAPTOR.

Dash Dinomouse
QUALITIES: HE IS THE STONE-AGE CHAMPION OF THE DINORACE GRAND PRIX.
AUTOSAURUS: A HIGH-ENERGY SPEEDSAURUS 3000.

CHASE AND LUCKY LIZARD

QUALITIES: THESE BROTHERS ALWAYS STICK TOGETHER.
AUTOSAURUS: A SUPERSIZED AUTOSAURUS XXL.

GUS GRANITE

QUALITIES: HE'S GOT ROCK-HARD DETERMINATION AND A PASSION FOR RACING.
AUTOSAURUS: A ROAD RACER WHO STOMPS ON THE COMPETITION.

Jack Pronto

QUALITIES: HE ONLY SLEEPS TWO HOURS A DAY AND SPENDS THE REST OF THE TIME RIDING HIS AUTOSAURUS.

AUTOSAURUS: AN AGILE SPORTASAURUS.

TINA SCURRYTAIL AND GINA SPRINTSTONE

QUALITIES: THESE BEST FRIENDS ARE OFF-ROAD-RACING CHAMPIONS!

AUTOSAURUS: A RALLYSAURUS WHO CAN HANDLE ROUGH TERRAIN.

Trap and Geronimo Stiltonoot

QUALITIES: MEMBERS OF THE ADVENTUROUS STILTONOOT FAMILY.

AUTOSAURUS: A LAZY CITY AUTOSAURUS.

. . . GO!

All of the competitors **stampeded** out of Old Mouse City. Their autosauruses kicked up a thick cloud of dust behind them as they ran toward Boulder Bay.

All of the competitors . . . *except us*, of course! My autosaurus got **SPOOKED** by the crowd and began to **spin** in circles. The race had just begun and we were already in last place.

When my autosaurus finally managed to pull himself together, we slowly headed out on the **ROCKY** path outside the city walls.

Up ahead we could see Thea and Dash

Dinomouse at the head of the race, on the plateau leading to the **Cheddar Volcano**. They looked like **tiny dots** in the distance! The other racers were NOT FAR behind them: the Lizard brothers, Tina and Gina, Jack Pronto, and Gus Granite.

Onward!

Trap started to complain.

"GET GOING, GERONIMO! MOVE THIS BIG OLD LUG!"

But my autosaurus was having a **hard time** carrying both of us. He **slowly** plodded along. **BONES AND STONES**, we would never catch up!

You've finally met your match!

See you at the finish line!

RODEO AT DINO RIVER!

We traveled for hours under the *BURNING SUN*. Finally, we reached the first stop on our journey: the Dino River! We would have to travel across the shallow part of the **water** to continue.

By that point, I felt like I was going to turn into a PUDDLE of melted cheese!

"It's so H©+," I complained. "And I can't even see the others. We might as well . . ."

Suddenly, my autosaurus *LURCHED* forward.

SPLAAASHHH!

Trap and I fell off his back and into the river! My autosaurus started to **guzzle** gallons and gallons of **water**. He must have been so **thirsty** after walking in that hot sun!

As my autosaurus quenched his thirst, Trap and I stayed in the river and **cooled off**. We knew we were in **LAST** place, but we couldn't go anywhere until our autosaurus

was done drinking anyway. As we dried off, I **ETCHED** the first two lines of my article into a **STONE** tablet.

Suddenly, the sound of wailing mice filled the air . . .

WAAAAH! WAAAAH!

"Trap! It sounds like someone is in **trouble**!" I said.

We followed the **SOBS** until we discovered the two mice on the riverbank.

It was **TiNA SCURRYTAIL** and **GiNA SPRINTSTONE**! The road rally champions were both looking upset.

"What's the matter?" I asked. "You should be miles ahead of us by now."

"It's our **Rallysaurus**," Gina replied with a sniff. "He abandoned us."

"He loves long road races," Tina said. "But he has a really **PLAYFUL** side, too. When he saw the **FISH** in the river he threw us off the saddle!"

"He ditched us so he could **play** with the fish," Gina explained.

I followed her gaze. The Rallysaurus was **SPLASHING** around in the water with the fish, just like a happy **baby** dinosaur.

I felt bad for Gina and Tina, and my **helpful** nature took over.

Waaah!

Waaah!

"Trap!" I exclaimed. "Let's lasso that Rallysaurus!"

Trap frowned. "**NO, NO, NO!** We are not a rescue team. Don't you see that this is an opportunity for us? If we leave now, we won't be in **LAST PLACE** anymore!"

I couldn't believe my cousin.

"Is that how you want to **Win**?" I asked him.

Trap shrugged. "Why not?"

"Listen up, Trap," I said, fuming. "**YOU** are the one who dragged me into this. **YOU** made me bring my autosaurus. There is no way I am going to turn my tail on rodents who need help. So unless you want to go back to Old Mouse City **right now**, you will help me get that Rallysaurus. Do you **understand**?"

Trap held up his paws. "Okay! **Simmer down**, Cousin."

We climbed on my autosaurus and found a good spot on the riverbank. Trap used a thick rope to make a lasso. He swung it at the Rallysaurus.

Splash! Splash! Splash! He kept missing his target. Finally, the lasso slipped around the beast's neck.

Tina and Gina jumped on the back of the Rallysaurus as soon as Trap PULLED him out of the river.

"Thanks a lot!" they shouted. Then the Rallysaurus ran off and disappeared into the distance.

"I knew it!" Trap yelled. "Now we're in LAST PLACE again! This stinks worse than moldy cheese!"

Trap was right; we had lost our chance to get ahead. But I was really happy that we helped Tina and Gina. I might be a

scaredy-mouse most of the time, but when a rodent needs **help** I will always lend a paw.

And so we got back into the race, tired, SOAKING WET, and . . .

ONCE AGAIN
IN LAST PLACE!

SQUISH! SQUISH! SQUISH!

Once we crossed the Dino River, the path was **ROCKY** but very flat. My autosaurus plodded along with the speed of a tired snail. Every so often, I leaned over and fed him some super-fruity smoothie with onion juice.

I was glad I had brought a lot of smoothie with me. Without it, we would risk getting stuck in this **unknown land** full of who-knows-what

TERRIFYING DANGERS!

Speaking of **unknown lands** . . . I didn't even know where we were! We could have been close to the camp of **TIGER KHAN'S** ferocious gang of tigers! Just the thought made my **FUR** stand on end.

Squeak!

Trap was complaining about my **SLOW** autosaurus when we reached an area of **GIANT RED ROCKS**. The path led to a massive crack that had **SPLIT** one rock in half.

The path continued right through the **NARROW** crack in the rock. We slipped through it and entered a canyon with **STEEP** walls. My autosaurus trotted through the **muddy** ground, his feet squishing with every step.

SQUISH! SQUISH! SQUISH!

He was moving even more **slowly** than before! But there was one good thing about the canyon — it was **SHADY** and **COOL**.

We hadn't traveled far when we came to an **amazing** sight: the **LIZARD BROTHERS**, perched on their Autosaurus XXL. He was stuck in the **mud** and couldn't get free!

"YES!"

Trap rejoiced. "We can pass them!"

But I looked at those poor rodents **STUCK** in that mud, alone and in

TROUBLE, and I couldn't just abandon them!

"Come on, Trap," I said. "Let's pull them out!"

Trap shook his head. "**Are you kidding?** Didn't we learn our lesson with Tina and Gina? Once we free the Lizard brothers, they will *RACE* ahead of us!"

"Listen, Cousin," I said firmly. "This is my autosaurus, so I am the one who calls the shots. Either we do as I say, or we return home **iM-ME-Di-ATE-LY**!"

Trap knew he couldn't argue with me, and he gave in.

We tied a rope around the Autosaurus XXL, and thanks to the **POWERFUL** (but slow) legs of my autosaurus, we pulled them out of that **slushy** sludge. Then Trap untied the rope, and we prepared to continue down the path to **BOULDER BAY**.

Chase Lizard gave me a big pat on the back. "**Thanks, pals!** We never would have made it without you two!"

Lucky Lizard nodded. "When we see you at the finish line, we will give you **five shells** each to make things even!"

Then the two brothers **SPED OFF** on their Autosaurus XXL, leaving us several

It's moving!

Keep pulling!

HUNDRED tails behind.

Bones and stones, was Trap **cheesed off** at me!

"We're in last place again," he **complained**. "And once more, it's your fault!"

While he was **sulking**, he decided not to speak to me — which really wasn't so bad.

Huff!

Come on!

FOSSILIZED FETA, I WAS REALLY TIRED OF LISTENING TO HIM COMPLAIN SO MUCH!

We got **going** again, but at this rate we wouldn't finish the *RACE* until the end of the Stone Age!

66

GLUUUB!

After the canyon, we reached **THE FOREST OF CARNIVOROUS PLANTS**! These plants had TEETH and **FANGS** and were ready to bite into the first mouse that passed by. I shivered in fear just thinking about it!

"You're just a scaredy-mouse," Trap scolded, seeing me tremble like a forest fern in a breeze. "We just have to stick to the center of the path, and the plants won't be able to reach us!"

I anxiously looked around. "Maybe so, but I still don't feel safe," I said.

The FOREST seemed to go on and on. I thought we would never get through it!

We followed the path as it snaked through the thick woods like a serpent. I kept a tight rein on the autosaurus so we wouldn't get near those mouse-munching plants.

But then I noticed that the plants didn't seem to want to get near us. HOW strange ... My thoughts were interrupted by a cry coming from the **THICK** of the forest.

"AAAAAAAAAAH!"

"That's the cry of a dinosaur!" said my autosaurus.

It was the **FIRST** time he had spoken during the whole trip! He is a dinosaur of few words.

We plodded on through the forest, but the SCREAMING did not stop. Then we discovered the source of the painful cries.

They came from **GUS GRANITE'S** Road Racer and Jack Pronto's Sportsaurus. The carnivorous plants were BITING the ankles of the poor beasts! The dinosaurs couldn't move because the plants' STICKY tongues were holding them.

"AAAAAAAAAAAAH!"

they yelled.

My autosaurus spoke up. "I'll handle

this," he said firmly. Then he very **calmly** approached the attacking plants.

He stopped a few steps short of the plants. Then he opened his **MOUTH** and greeted them.

"HELLOOOOO!"

His **rotten** breath, fueled by the **ONIONS** in his super-fruity smoothie, floated over the plants like a stinky cloud.

"Gluuub! Ewww!" the plants cried.

The horrible smell made the plants **shrivel** right up! Their **STICKY** tongues lost their grips on the Road Racer and the Sportsaurus. Gus Granite and Jack Pronto were **FREE** to race!

That's when I realized that the reason the **CARNIVOROUS PLANTS** had left Trap and me alone was because of the **disgusting** breath of my autosaurus. The

super-fruity smoothies had saved us!

One of the plants got angry. "You've got **SWAMP BREATH**, you ugly beast!" it yelled.

"*I'm* **ugly**? Have you looked in a mirror lately?" asked the autosaurus, **BLOWING** his breath at the plant again.

The plant shrank back, **HORRIFIED**.

Take pity on us!

"**ACK!** Take pity on us!" it begged. "If you close your mouth, I promise that I will never BITE an autosaurus again in my life!"

Satisfied, my autosaurus stomped back onto the path.

"**Thank you!**" said Gus Granite.

"Yes, thanks!" added Jack Pronto.

The two racers were busy BANDAGING the ankles of their autosauruses. We left them behind as we headed toward Boulder Bay.

For the FiRST time, we weren't in LAST place! Trap had nothing to complain about. (Except maybe about having to smell the BAD BREATH of my autosaurus!)

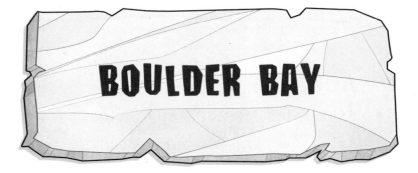

BOULDER BAY

We climbed a hill and, at the top, we saw that we were looking down on **BOULDER BAY**! We had arrived at our final destination!

I had been expecting a **DARK**, scary-looking place. But the scene before me was **enchanting**. The hill sloped down toward the sea into a cove of sparkling blue water. Dotting the grassy slope were many small, shrubby **PLANTS** loaded with bright red fruit: **hot lava peppers**!

Trap and I climbed off

the autosaurus and started picking as many **peppers** as we could. After a few hours my paws began to **ache** so I decided to sit and work on my article. I sat under the **SHADE** of a tree and began to etch the latest events onto a stone tablet.

I worked until Trap called out to me.

"Look over there, Geronimo!"

A black cloud was **SWIFTLY** approaching from across the cove. Was it a **storm**? Then we heard a loud **buzzing** sound, and we knew what we were up against.

"*SAND BITERS!*" Trap yelled.

Sand biters are tiny but **AGGRESSIVE** insects! Trap and I ran as fast as we could, but the **LITTLE BUGS** caught up to us.

They started to BITE us right through our fur! OUCH!

BONES AND STONES, HOW ITCHY!

HOW ANNOYING!

And most of all . . . HOW PAINFUL!

"Run for the water!" Trap yelled, but there was one **problem** — we couldn't move more than a paw in front of us, because the bugs surrounded us. There was **NO ESCAPE**!

Suddenly, the sound of a piercing whistle hit our ears.

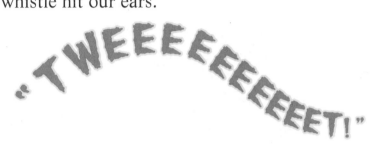

"TWEEEEEEEEEEET!"

The swarm of sand biters parted for a moment.

When Trap and I lifted our heads, we saw an ANCIENT RODENT with a long beard standing on a rock, whistling.

Called by the whistle, two flying creatures swooped down into the bay. They were pterodactyls, with SHARP claws and teeth!

"CAWWW! CAWWW!"

they shrieked.

HOW TERRIFYING!

Trap and I jumped behind some bushes to **HIDE**, but we quickly realized that the pterodactyls weren't interested in us. They were after the sand biters! The scared biting bugs fled.

Scratching our bug bites, Trap and I stood up.

"I'm guessing that you two are contestants in that race," said the rodent with the **GRAY** beard.

"Yes," I admitted.

"**I knew it!**" said the rodent. "You are the fifth team that I have **saved** from the sand biters!"

Trap and I LOOKED at each other, surprised.

"The fifth?" I asked the old rodent.

"Yes," he answered. "My name is Pablo Pepperpaws and I have lived in this bay for so long that I don't even remember how

old I am! But I remember the four teams that came before you."

"**FOUR TEAMS!** We'll never catch up," Trap cried.

"I told them all a **Shortcut** to Old Mouse City," Pablo said. "I can tell you, too, if you like."

"**Yes!**" Trap and I cried.

He told us, and we thanked him. We knew we were **FAR BEHIND** four other teams. But the *RACE* wasn't over yet!

HUFF! HUFF! HUFF!

"Run as *FAST* as you can!" I told my autosaurus as Trap and I climbed back on board.

But the poor dinosaur was **exhausted**, and I was almost out of smoothie! So he **plodded** on more slowly than before.

"We'll never reach the other teams," Trap complained.

We traveled out of the bay, through a low **jungle**, and then emerged into a strange **WHITE LAND**. The whiteness stretched out in all directions, and there was no sign of **LIFE** anywhere.

"What is this place?" I asked, **sweating**

under the hot prehistoric sun.

The autosaurus stopped and licked the ground.

"Hey!" he exclaimed. "This is salt. We've ended up in a SALT DESERT!"

Trap lost all hope at that moment. "We'll

Waaah!

never make it now! Good-bye, victory! Good-bye, Volcanico! **Good-bye, shells!**"

"Calm down, Trap," I said. "Save your **energy**. You will need it to get across this salt desert!"

But Trap had given up. "**NO! NO!**" he yelled. "It's pointless! We'll never win now! **WAAAH, POOR ME!** And it's all your fault! You and your **superslow** autosaurus!"

My autosaurus looked back at Trap. "Oh yeah? Let's see *you* travel for **THOUSANDS** of tails with two rodents on your back! You'd take two steps and then **CRAWL** back into your cave with your tail between your legs!"

Trap didn't argue with that, and we

continued on. The white salt blinded our eyes, and the *BURNING* sun beat down on our fur.

"It's so hot that you could grill a CHEESE SANDWICH on this ground!" I remarked.

But the heat didn't seem to bother my autosaurus. He kept a **STEADY PACE** and never gave up.

Then I spotted something up ahead. There were Tina and Gina, followed by the Lizard brothers! We were gaining on them! Unlike my autosaurus, those dinosaurs were wilting in the heat. They were moving slower than prehistoric snails!

First we passed the Lizard brothers and their AUTOSAURUS XXL.

The GReen dinosaur's tongue was sticking out, and he was PANTING heavily.

HUFF! HUFF! HUFF!

Tina and Gina's **Rallysaurus** was **DRIPPING** with sweat and short of breath.

HUFF! HUFF! HUFF!

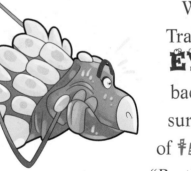

When we passed them, Trap couldn't believe his **EYES**. He kept looking back at them to make sure it wasn't some kind of **trick**.

"By the **GREAT ZAP**!" he exclaimed. "It feels like we're **flying** past them!"

When we finally made it out of the

SALT DESERT, we looked behind us. We couldn't even see Tina, Gina, and the Lizard brothers.

BOUNCING BOULDERS! We had been in last place for so long, and now we were in **THIRD PLACE**! There were only two *RACERS* in front of us: my sister, Thea Stiltonoot, and the great champion Dash Dinomouse . . .

THE GROWLING TIGER DOESN'T BITE!

WE HAD ALMOST DONE IT!

All we had to do was catch up to Thea and Dash Dinomouse before the **finish line**! I felt like winning was within our paws.

"You can do it!" I told my autosaurus, when he stopped SUDDENLY, nearly throwing us from the saddle.

SCREEECH!

The road ended at the edge of a very TALL, very *STEEP* cliff!

We leaned over and looked down into a **DEEP GORGE**. To our surprise, we saw

THEA and **Dash** —
and they were in big
TROUBLE! They were
tied like string
cheese to the trunk
of a prehistoric palm
tree.

Those poor rodents
had fallen into the
clutches of TIGER
KHAN! He was the

There's no
escape!

Growl!

number one enemy of all cavemice and the leader of the fierce SABER-TOOTHED SQUAD — and he had captured my sister and Dash!

Helpless and afraid, the two mice were moments away from becoming dinner for a horde of HUNGRY saber-toothed tigers!

Tiger Khan's warriors, meanwhile, were (unsuccessfully) *CHASING* Thea's Velociraptor, GRUNTY, and Dash's Speedsaurus 3000.

Help!

"Once we capture your dinosaurs, we'll take you to our camp for a nice dinner," Tiger Khan snarled to Thea and Dash. "And you will be the **MAIN COURSE**! Mwah, ha, ha!"

BONES AND STONES! WE HAD TO HELP THEM, FAST!

But what could two rodents do against a horde of cats with **SHARP FANGS**?

Suddenly, my autosaurus spoke up.

"**LEAVE IT TO ME!**" he growled.

I had never seen such a *MENACING* look on his face!

"Climb off me!" he ordered, and we scrambled down.

Then he stomped toward a **LARGE BOULDER** on the edge of the cliff. He pressed his back against the rock and began to *PUSH* with all his **might**.

I couldn't believe my eyes! Underneath my autosaurus's big belly were some **massive muscles**!

Trap lent a **PAW**, and the two managed to push the **HUGE BOULDER** off the cliff. It rolled down toward the tigers.

The **RUMBLING** sound caught the

attention of Tiger Khan and his warriors.

"AAAAAH! SAVE YOURSELVES!"

a tiger yelled, and the others joined in, SCREAMING and running away. TERRORIZED by the landslide of earth and stones, the entire Saber-Toothed Squad fled with their paws up. Even Grunty and the Speedsaurus 3000 fled the scene to avoid being **crushed**.

Thea and Dash, thankfully, were safe, protected by the **indestructible** trunk of the prehistoric **palm tree** they were tied to. My autosaurus must have known this when he started the landslide.

GREAT ROCKY BOULDERS! HE WAS SMARTER THAN I THOUGHT!

When the landslide ended, my autosaurus **JUMPED** off the cliff with unexpected agility. Trap and I ran after him and *RACED* toward the two prisoners. We quickly untied the ropes and **FREED** Thea and Dash. As they thanked us, Grunty and the Speedsaurus 3000 returned. There was no time to waste — the **TIGERS** could return at any moment!

So we all climbed on our dinosaurs and took off toward *Old Mouse City*. Behind us, we heard Tiger Khan shout, "**YOU WILL PAY FOR THIS, YOU ROTTEN CAVE RATS!**"

"We're not afraid, you **BIG BULLY**!" Trap yelled back. "You're all **growl** and no **BITE**!"

Luckily, Tiger Khan didn't come after us. As we made our way back home, I thought about all the **OBSTACLES** we had overcome. We had RESCUED all of the other contestants, we had been attacked by flies, and we had suffered through the heat, yet we had still moved from last place to third place!

Thea and Dash were already ahead of us, but that was okay. Even if we didn't cross the FINISH LINE first, we were still winners!

THANKS, THEA! YOU'RE THE BEST!

The rest of the race continued **smoothly**. We didn't face any other **DANGERS**. We didn't encounter any contestants in trouble. Before we knew it, we had arrived at the finish line in **Singing Rock Square**!

Up ahead, we could see that Dash Dinomouse was about to cross the finish line. Just before he did, Grunty **DARTED** ahead of the Speedsaurus 3000 with **LIGHTNING SPEED**! Thea **won** the race!

Dash took **SECOND** place, and Trap and I arrived in **THIRD**.

The crowd at the finish line greeted us

more WARMLY than a cauldron of **melted fondue**. They cheered for all the contestants, even the ones who arrived much **later** than we did: Chase and Lucky Lizard, Tina Scurrytail and Gina Sprintstone, Gus Granite, and Jack Pronto.

Every one of us was exhausted, **dirty**, SWEATY, STARVING, and thirsty . . . but it felt amazing to have finished that **DANGEROUS** race without harming a strand of fur!

Trap was disappointed that we didn't win, but he accepted our third-place finish with real sportmouseship. He happily shook the 🐾🐾🐾🐾 of the other contestants.

At the awards ceremony, Sunny Rottencheese thanked all of us for bringing her the **lava peppers**. She promised to give all of the contestants a round of Volcanico when it was finished. **YUM!**

Then Ernest Heftymouse presented Thea with the first prize: a sack of **five hundred shells** to spend at the Rottencheese cheese shop! She hoisted it into the air VICTORIOUSLY, and the crowd cheered.

"HOORAY FOR THEA!"

Victory!

But Thea asked everyone to quiet down so she could speak.

"**Citizens of Old Mouse City!**" she began solemnly. "Now that I have won the race, I would like to do something that I think you will all agree with."

Everyone was as **quiet** as a, well . . . a **quiet mouse** . . . waiting to hear what she would say next.

"Without the *generous* help of my brother, Geronimo Stiltonoot, none of us would have finished this race. Not even me!" she exclaimed.

The crowd **gasped**.

"What do you mean?" asked Ernest.

Thea *smiled* and looked at me.

"During the race, each contestant fell into **DANGER**," she explained. "And Geronimo **helped** us all. If it weren't for

him, not one of us would have reached this FINISH LINE. This is why Geronimo and Trap deserve **FiRSt PRiZe**!"

The crowd was **silent** for a moment. Then Dash Dinomouse shouted:

"HOORAY FOR GERONIMO!
HOORAY FOR TRAP!"

He began to applaud, and the other contestants joined in. Soon the whole crowd was **cheering** for me.

I was really touched by what Thea did! I am **lucky** to have such a special sister.

"Thanks, Thea," I said. "Your offer is very generous. And in that spirit, I will give my half of the shells to Trap, so he can carry out his **DREAM** of stocking the Rotten Tooth Tavern with a year's worth of cheese!"

Trap threw his paws around my neck and almost **crushed** me, he was so happy!

"But Trap, you must promise me one thing," I added after he loosened his grasp on me. "From now on, once a week, you will invite me, Thea, and all the other contestants of this incredible race to your tavern for **dinner**!"

"Consider it done, cousin!" he said,

shaking my paw.

"And the dinner will also include a meal for my **AUTOSAURUS**, who is the true hero of this story!" I added.

"Of course!" agreed Trap, and he ran to hug my autosaurus. The dinosaur shook his head.

"You cavemice really are strange!" he said.

THE GREATEST RACE IN PREHISTORY!

A few **EVENINGS** later, we all met at the Rotten Tooth Tavern to celebrate finishing the race. Clarissa (my crush) joined us as well.

Trap and Greasella prepared dozens of delicious dishes for us, and we ate every crumb! Then Sunny Rottencheese brought a surprise to our table: the first batch of **VOLCANICO** she had made with the lava peppers we had brought back from Boulder Bay. It was mousetastic!

We ate Volcanico until we were full and then finished off the meal with some mammoth milkshakes. (Clarissa likes **vanilla** best, just like I do!)

When the meal was finally over, Trap and I slipped away to the **warehouse** behind the restaurant. I had a **SURPRISE** for everyone. When Trap and I returned, we were holding several heavy **STONE TABLETS** in our paws.

Our friends eyed us *curiously* as we entered.

"**Friends!**" I exclaimed. "As you know, Ernest Heftymouse, our village leader, asked me to **ETCH** an article about this race."

Thea clapped her paws together. "Is this the article?"

"I did **MUCH MORE** than an article," I revealed. "I started writing the article, but I couldn't **S+⊚P**. I wrote word after word, sentence after sentence, chapter after chapter . . . and the result was a **MOUNTAIN** of etched tablets. And here they are!"

Everyone clapped.

"This story is dedicated to Sunny Rottencheese and all of you who took part in this adventure," I told them.

So there you have it, my dear rodent friends. In the TABLETS I gave to my fellow contestants, I etched **everything you have just read**! The entire tale!

I hope you enjoyed it, just as I hope you like the *dedication* I wrote at the end . . .

TO SUNNY ROTTENCHEESE, TO ALL THE CONTESTANTS IN THE RACE, AND TO ALL OF MY WONDERFUL

CAVEMOUSE READERS . . . WITH MY BEST STONE AGE WISHES!

Geronimo Stiltonoot

Don't miss any adventures of the cavemice!

#1 The Stone of Fire

#2 Watch Your Tail!

#3 Help, I'm in Hot Lava!

#4 The Fast and the Frozen

#5 The Great Mouse Race

#6 Don't Wake the Dinosaur!

#7 I'm a Scaredy-Mouse!

#8 Surfing for Secrets

#9 Get the Scoop, Geronimo!

#10 My Autosaurus Will Win!

#11 Sea Monster Surprise

Be sure to read all my fabumouse adventures!

#21 The Wild, Wild West

#22 The Secret of Cacklefur Castle

A Christmas Tale

#23 Valentine's Day Disaster

#24 Field Trip to Niagara Falls

#25 The Search for Sunken Treasure

#26 The Mummy with No Name

#27 The Christmas Toy Factory

#28 Wedding Crasher

#29 Down and Out Down Under

#30 The Mouse Island Marathon

#31 The Mysterious Cheese Thief

Christmas Catastrophe

#32 Valley of the Giant Skeletons

#33 Geronimo and the Gold Medal Mystery

#34 Geronimo Stilton, Secret Agent

#35 A Very Merry Christmas

#36 Geronimo's Valentine

#37 The Race Across America

#38 A Fabumouse School Adventure

#39 Singing Sensation

#40 The Karate Mouse

#41 Mighty Mount Kilimanjaro

#42 The Peculiar Pumpkin Thief

#43 I'm Not a Supermouse!

#44 The Giant Diamond Robbery

#45 Save the White Whale!

#46 The Haunted Castle

#47 Run for the Hills, Geronimo!

#48 The Mystery in Venice

#49 The Way of the Samurai

#50 This Hotel Is Haunted!

#51 The Enormouse Pearl Heist

#52 Mouse in Space!

#53 Rumble in the Jungle

#54 Get into Gear, Stilton!

#55 The Golden Statue Plot

#56 Flight of the Red Bandit

The Hunt for the Golden Book

#57 The Stinky Cheese Vacation

#58 The Super Chef Contest

#59 Welcome to Moldy Manor

The Hunt for the Curious Cheese

#60 The Treasure of Easter Island

#61 Mouse House Hunter

#62 Mouse Overboard!

The Hunt for the Secret Papyrus

#63 The Cheese Experiment

MEET GERONIMO STILTONIX

He is a spacemouse — the Geronimo Stilton of a parallel universe! He is captain of the spaceship *MouseStar 1*. While flying through the cosmos, he visits distant planets and meets crazy aliens. His adventures are out of this world!

#1 Alien Escape

#2 You're Mine, Captain!

#3 Ice Planet Adventure

#4 The Galactic Goal

#5 Rescue Rebellion

#6 The Underwater Planet

#7 Beware! Space Junk!

Don't miss any of these exciting Thea Sisters adventures!

Thea Stilton and the Dragon's Code

Thea Stilton and the Mountain of Fire

Thea Stilton and the Ghost of the Shipwreck

Thea Stilton and the Secret City

Thea Stilton and the Mystery in Paris

Thea Stilton and the Cherry Blossom Adventure

Thea Stilton and the Star Castaways

Thea Stilton: Big Trouble in the Big Apple

Thea Stilton and the Ice Treasure

Thea Stilton and the Secret of the Old Castle

Thea Stilton and the Blue Scarab Hunt

Thea Stilton and the Prince's Emerald

Thea Stilton and the Mystery on the Orient Express

Thea Stilton and the Dancing Shadows

Thea Stilton and the Legend of the Fire Flowers

Thea Stilton and the Spanish Dance Mission

Thea Stilton and the Journey to the Lion's Den

Thea Stilton and the Great Tulip Heist

Thea Stilton and the Chocolate Sabotage

Thea Stilton and the Missing Myth

Thea Stilton and the Lost Letters

Thea Stilton and the Tropical Treasure

Thea Stilton and the Hollywood Hoax

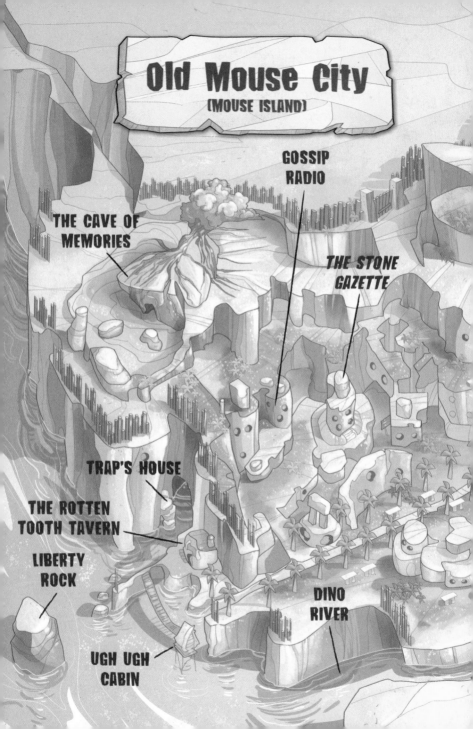